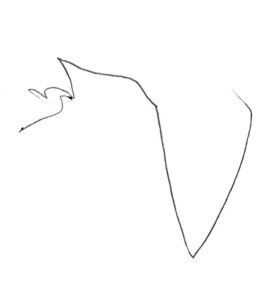

This

The Bear with Sticky Paws

book belongs to:

. . . .

KEEP YOUR PAWS OFF!

for Martha,
with love 🐾

and for my small friend
Conrad
🐾

tiger tales
an imprint of ME Media, LLC
202 Old Ridgefield Road, Wilton, CT 06897
This paperback edition published 2009
Published in hardcover in the United States 2008
Originally published in Great Britain 2007
by Orchard Press
Text and illustrations copyright ©2007 Clara Vulliamy
CIP data is available
ISBN-13: 978-1-58925-070-3 (hardcover)
ISBN-10: 1-58925-070-2 (hardcover)
ISBN-13: 978-1-58925-413-8 (paperback)
ISBN-10: 1-58925-413-9 (paperback)
Printed in China
1 3 5 7 9 10 8 6 4 2

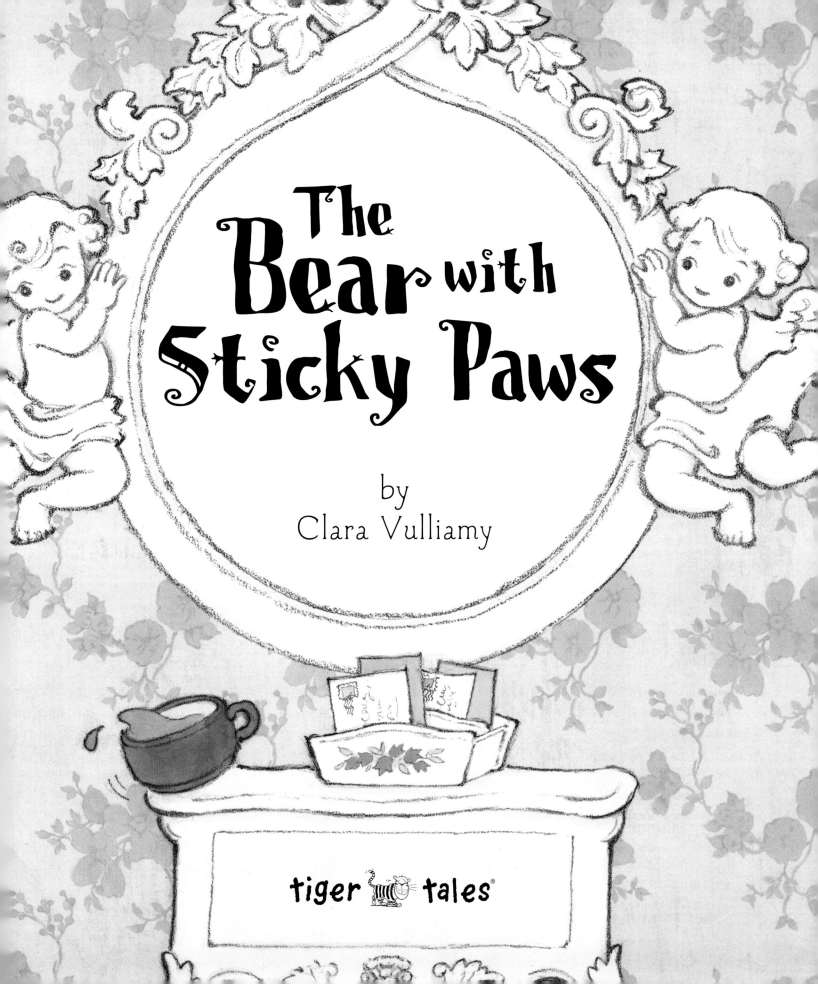

The Bear with Sticky Paws

by

Clara Vulliamy

tiger tales

There's a girl named Lily
and she's being very grumpy,
stamping her little feet and
slamming the door.

   She says,

"I don't want all this **breakfast!**"

and throws down her spoon.

"**NO**, I won't wash my face.
NO, I won't brush my hair.
NO, I won't get dressed ..."

"NO! NO! NO! NO! NO! NO! NO! NO!"

Until Mom calls out,

"*Stop!*"

And—

oh NO!

Mom's leaving!

But then,

ding-dong!

At the door is a bear, a small, white, fluffy one, standing on his suitcase to reach the bell.

"Breakfast?" says the bear, sniffing the air.

"BREAKFAST?
Yes, please!"

The bear eats it all.
"MORE!"
says the bear.

Lily makes

5 pancakes,

8 pieces of toast with jam,

and 9 bowls of oatmeal.

And—oh NO!

Sticky paws everywhere!

But the bear
doesn't care. . . .
"Let's PLAY!"
says the bear.

He's
snuffling
and sniffling . . .

hiding
and sliding,

leaping
and climbing!

And—
oh NO!

He's on top of the furniture!

"Lunchtime!" calls Lily.
"UP HERE!" says the bear.
So Lily has to throw the food up to him—

7 slices of pizza,

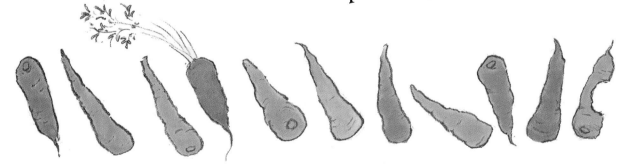

11 carrots,

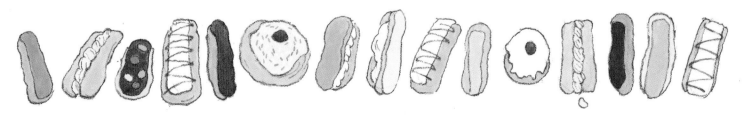

and 15 doughnuts.

"Let's dress up!" says the bear.
"Okay," says Lily.
And—oh NO!

Down comes the curtain.

"PRETTY!"
says the bear.
And—oh NO!
He's found Mom's
stuff, too.

"We'd better play outside," says Lily.

"SWIM!" says the bear.

And—

oh NO!

He jumps right in the fountain.

Lily serves snacks. There are

9 honey sandwiches,

11 bowls of milk,

and too many ice-cream treats to count.

"I'm tired," says Lily.

"NOT TIRED!" says the bear.

"Come on," says Lily,
taking him by a sticky paw.
"It's your bedtime."

"No," says the bear.

"**NO**, I don't want a bath.
NO, I hate being brushed.
NO, I won't go to bed…"

Until Lily calls out . . .

"STOP!"

"What about this mess?" says Lily.

"MESS?" says the bear.

"I don't know!

I've got to go!

GOOD-BYE!"

Out goes the bear.
And—

oh NO!

In comes *Mom!*

"What about this mess?" asks Mom.

And Lily says,
     "I will clean it up.
          I will wash my face.
               I will brush my hair...."

And Lily has all she
really wants—

One lovely Mom,
one huge hug,
and one big kiss.